Arthur Accused!

A Marc Brown **ARTHUR** Chapter Book

Arthur Accused!

Little, Brown and Company

Boston   New York   London

First Edition

The characters and events portrayed in this book are fictitious. Any similarity to real persons, living or dead, is coincidental and not intended by the author.

Arthur® is a registered trademark of Marc Brown.

Text by Stephen Krensky, based on the teleplay by James Greenberg
Text has been reviewed and assigned a reading level by Laurel S. Ernst, M.A., Teachers College, Columbia, University, New York, New York; reading specialist, Chappaqua, New York

0-316-12150-9

Library of Congress Catalog Card Number 97-075722

10 9 8 7 6 5 4 3 2

WOR (HC)
COM-MO (PB)

Printed in the United States of America

For my grandma Thora,
who would be so proud

Chapter 1

Hello, stranger. I'm Buster Baxter, private eye. You can call me Buster for short. I'm going to tell you about my first case. It involved my pal Arthur, some missing quarters, and a whole lot of trouble.

The whole thing started two days ago. It was an ordinary Wednesday — the kind that comes right between Tuesday and Thursday. The middle of the week, when anything can happen — and usually does.

The school day had just ended, and Arthur was standing in the school hallway behind a long table. In front of him was a bowl half-filled with quarters.

"Help the fire department buy a new puppy!" Arthur called. "Only a quarter!"

A couple of kids dropped in quarters.

"Thanks," said Arthur. "Thanks a lot."

Binky Barnes walked up to him. His head and shoulders blocked the light from the hall window. "What's with the bowl, Arthur?"

"I'm collecting money for Mrs. MacGrady's fund drive. We're going to buy a puppy for the fire department." He showed Binky a picture.

"That dog has a lot of spots. You sure it isn't sick?"

"No, no. Dalmatians all look like that. So what do you think? How about a quarter?"

Binky considered it. He weighed the thought of a shiny quarter against a little dalmatian puppy. The puppy in his head

rolled over and made little snuffling sounds. It sat up and wagged its tail. The quarter just sat there being shiny.

"Here," said Binky. He reached into his pocket and flipped a quarter into the bowl. "There's just one thing," he added, glaring at Arthur.

"What's that?"

"Don't tell anybody I gave. It's bad for my image."

"Okay," said Arthur.

Binky seemed satisfied, at least for the moment.

"Hey, Arthur!" yelled Buster as he ran down the hall.

"What's with the goofy hat?" asked Arthur.

"This hat is not goofy," said Buster. "It's a fedora — part of my new detective kit. I've been snooping — ah, looking for crimes."

"Have you found any?"

4

"No." Buster pushed back the brim of his hat. "But I did pick up some secret information."

He peered to the left and right, making sure no one else was listening.

"You promise this will go no further?"

Arthur nodded.

Buster leaned forward. "Third-grade picnic this Friday," he whispered.

Arthur rolled his eyes. "I know that, Buster. There have been signs up for two weeks."

"Oh. Well, I was half right. It's still information. Anyway, I'm not giving up. I'll find a crime. Maybe I'll find one at the arcade. My mom's taking me there this afternoon. Want to come?"

Most of the kids seemed to have gone home. Arthur figured he had probably collected all the quarters he was going to get for the day. And the arcade was a great place.

"Sure," he said. "Just let me take these quarters to Mrs. MacGrady."

He emptied the quarters from the bowl into a paper bag.

"I'll go find my mom outside," said Buster. "We'll wait for you. Hurry!"

Arthur nodded and ran down the hall.

Chapter 2

· · · · · · · · · · ·

I wasn't with Arthur for the next few minutes. Maybe if I had been, he wouldn't have had any problems. But as it says in the Detective's Handbook, *When life takes a wrong turn, just try not to get lost.*

Arthur hurried to the cafeteria kitchen. He could tell that Mr. Morris, the janitor, had cleaned the floors since lunch. "Clean enough to eat off of," Mr. Morris liked to say, but Arthur preferred plates.

Mrs. MacGrady was on the phone.

"What's that, Chief? Have you thought of a name yet?"

Arthur waved, trying to get her attention. He didn't want to keep Buster and his mother waiting.

But Mrs. MacGrady didn't see him.

"Smokey. Sure, that's a nice name for a dog. I see, I see . . ."

Arthur tried to be patient. On the counter next to him were some baking ingredients. There were bags of flour and sugar, sticks of butter, eggs, and chocolate squares.

"Where there's Smokey, there's a firefighter. Cute, Chief. Very cute. I just don't want the dog to get a complex. Dogs are sensitive, you know."

The bag was getting heavy in Arthur's hand. He went to put it down and accidentally knocked over the bag of flour.

"Chester's a fine name for a dog, don't you think? My first husband was named Chester."

Since Mrs. MacGrady still wasn't watching, Arthur was able to clean up the flour without her seeing him. Some of it had gotten into the bag of quarters, but that was okay because flour wouldn't do the quarters any harm.

Arthur looked at the clock. He had been standing there for more than five minutes.

"Mrs. MacGrady? Excuse me, Mrs. MacGrady?" He held up the bag of quarters.

She waved her hand, although whether she was waving to Arthur or making motions to the phone, it was hard to know.

"I'm just leaving —," Arthur began.

But Mrs. MacGrady, still talking on the phone, had turned away.

Arthur couldn't wait any longer. If he did, Buster would have a fit. Mrs. MacGrady was bound to be off the phone soon.

"I'm leaving the bag on the counter," Arthur called out. "Right here, next to the flour."

Then he left.

Chapter 3

· · · · · · · · · · ·

When Arthur and I arrived at the arcade, I had two things on my mind. One was the games themselves. I wanted a return match with Alien Explorer, *which had roughed me up the last time. That game needed to be taught a lesson. And I was just the one to do it.*

The other thing on my mind was finding a mystery to solve. Arcades draw shifty characters the way a garbage dump draws flies. I figured something would come my way if I kept a good lookout.

"Buster," said Arthur, "what are you doing with that magnifying glass?"

"Just checking things out." Buster was peering closely at a table. "Some mysteries like to play hide-and-seek." He moved the glass back to Arthur, looking up and down. "Look at you, for example."

"What *about* me?" said Arthur.

"You've got white stuff on your clothes."

"I do not."

Buster looked closer. "Definitely some kind of powder."

Arthur looked down. There was a little . . . Suddenly he smiled. "Oh, that's no mystery. When I was dropping off the quarters in the cafeteria, I accidentally spilled some flour. It must have gotten on my shirt."

Buster looked disappointed. "Well, it *could* have been a mystery."

"Sorry," said Arthur. "Anyway, I thought we were here to play."

They made the rounds, playing some games themselves and watching others

play, too. Neither of them was very lucky at surviving *CrashCourse 2000* or getting through the night at *Haunted Hotel*, but Buster did better at *Alien Explorer*.

"Take that, you mangy mutant!" he cried. "Ah, revenge is sweet!" The mutant had always done him in before.

"Just a few more minutes, boys," Buster's mother called out to them. She was waiting for them outside the arcade.

Buster was out of money, but Arthur still had enough for one more game. He decided to try a pinball machine. He put in his quarters and pulled the knob. As he released it, the ball shot up the slot and around the ramp.

"Go, Arthur, go!" said Buster, who never had much luck at pinball.

The ball ricocheted around the platform. Whenever it lost speed and fell downward, Arthur caught it with the flipper and sent it up again.

"Whoa! That was close, Arthur! Keep it up."

As Arthur's score rose, the machine lit up in more and more colors. A crowd began to gather behind him.

"Watch out, there!"

"Hold it . . . now!"

Arthur was on a roll.

"Go for the spinner!"

Arthur did his best, but finally the third ball dodged the right flipper and sank into the hole.

"Arthur, you did it!" cried Buster. "You hit the high score!"

Arthur looked up. His 868,233 points were in first place. He even got to put his initials next to them.

"That score will stand forever," said Buster. He pounded Arthur on the back as the onlookers cheered.

When they left the arcade, Buster was

still excited. "My best friend hit the high score," he said proudly to one and all.

It wasn't the same as finding a mystery to solve, but it was still pretty good.

Chapter 4

• • • • • • • • • • •

As much as I hated to admit it, I was starting to feel a little down. Why was it so hard to find a mystery to investigate? Did all detectives have these problems? Still, at least I had some good news to share at school the next day.

"Step aside, everyone. Make way! Pinball wizard coming through."

Buster made these comments as he and Arthur walked down the hall.

"Buster, please!" said Arthur. "It's embarrassing."

"Don't be so modest, Arthur. You deserve the attention."

Arthur sighed.

"Nimble fingers here! Eyes like a hawk. Reflexes like a cat!"

As they passed the principal's office, Mr. Haney waved them in.

"Good morning, Arthur, Buster," he said. "Oh, Arthur, don't forget to give Mrs. MacGrady the quarters you collected for her fund drive."

"I already did, Mr. Haney."

The school secretary, Miss Tingley, frowned. "That's odd. She told me she never got them."

"Aha!" said Buster. "Maybe they were stolen."

"Buster, please contain yourself," said Mr. Haney. The principal turned to Arthur. "Is it possible you brought them home by mistake?"

"No," said Buster. "He came straight to the arcade with me. In fact, he did very well at pinball. You're looking at Mr. High Score."

"Really?" Mr. Haney frowned. Miss Tingley frowned, too.

"I got the high score once," Buster went on. "Cost me a fortune. Took all my birthday money. Like a hundred quarters. Boy, did I —"

Buster stopped suddenly. He stared at Arthur. So did Mr. Haney and Miss Tingley.

"What's the matter?" asked Arthur.

"We have a little mystery here," said Mr. Haney.

Miss Tingley frowned again. "Not so little," she said.

A short while later, Arthur found himself sitting in the principal's office. He felt very small. The chair he was sitting in was very uncomfortable.

"You were responsible for the money,"
Mr. Haney was saying.

"You certainly were," Miss Tingley
added.

Arthur shrank farther into the chair.

He looked from one stern face to the
other. "You mean . . . you think *I* stole the
quarters? But I left them on the cafeteria
counter."

"Well, Mrs. MacGrady never saw them,"
Mr. Haney said. "You were responsible for
them. If that money doesn't turn up, I'm
afraid you'll have to serve a day —"

Miss Tingley cleared her throat.

"I mean, a week of after-school detention." Mr. Haney paused. "And no third-
grade picnic for you tomorrow."

Arthur was horrified.

As he left the office, Buster rushed up
to him.

"So what happened?"

Arthur explained it to him. "My first

important job, and everyone thinks I'm a thief. But I'm innocent."

"Of course you are," said Buster. "That's why you need a detective. Like, say . . . me."

"I don't know, Buster. Do you really think you can find out what happened to the quarters?"

"No problem! I could solve this case in my sleep. Well, no, I guess I'd have to be awake. And not wearing my pajamas, either. But don't worry, Arthur. Buster Baxter is on the case. You'll be going to that picnic tomorrow. Trust me."

Arthur wanted to believe him, but he wished he felt more hopeful. "Okay, Buster, do your stuff. But promise me one thing."

"Sure. What is it?"

"Try not to get me into any deeper trouble than I'm in now. Things are bad enough as it is."

Chapter 5

• • • • • • • • • • •

In every case there's a key witness, and this case was no different. I knew who she was, and she knew who she was, too.

Last name: MacGrady.

First name: Mrs.

Occupation: Cafeteria lady.

Buster found Mrs. MacGrady in the cafeteria kitchen. She was mixing ingredients in a large bowl. He explained that he was investigating the disappearance of Arthur's quarters.

"Can you tell me your whereabouts yesterday afternoon?" he asked.

" 'Whereabouts,' huh? That's a pretty fancy way of asking me where I was. Well, I was right here in the kitchen, making brownies. Buster, keep your hands away from that bowl!"

"Aha!" said Buster, pulling back his hand. "Maybe I should taste this. It could be evidence."

Mrs. MacGrady waved a spatula at him. "Nice try. But you'll have to wait for the picnic like everyone else."

She moved over to a long table covered with tiny cherry tarts and began squirting whipped cream onto each one.

"I remember speaking to the chief. We had quite a long conversation. Then I made the brownies."

"Did you see Arthur?"

"No, I didn't see anyone all afternoon. Oh, wait, that's not true. Mr. Morris was here. My mixer jammed a few times, and the brownie mix overflowed onto the floor. He came in to mop up the mess."

"Hmmm," said Buster, popping one of the cherry tarts into his mouth.

"Maybe you should talk to Mr. Morris," Mrs. MacGrady suggested.

"Mank you fery huch," Buster mumbled, and ran out before she could say anything.

He found Mr. Morris, the school janitor, pushing a cart along the hallway.

"Excuse me, Mr. Morris," said Buster. "May I ask you a couple of questions?"

"Shoot."

Buster explained that he was trying to re-create the sequence of events from the previous afternoon.

" 'Sequence of events,' eh?" said Mr. Morris. "You sound like one of the those TV detective shows."

"Really?" said Buster. He beamed. Then he remembered that detectives don't beam and tried to look serious again.

"Tell me about yesterday."

"Well, let's see," said Mr. Morris. "I was in the teachers' room —"

"Aha!" said Buster suspiciously. "And *what* were you doing there?"

"Changing a lightbulb. Then I got the call to go to the kitchen. Seems Mrs. MacGrady was having some trouble with her mixer. When I got there, the floor was covered with brownie batter. So I cleaned up the mess."

Buster folded his arms. "And do you *always* clean up after Mrs. MacGrady?"

"No, not often. She's pretty tidy as a rule. But I was glad to help. Anything else?"

Buster wanted to think of more questions. He liked asking questions. But he couldn't think of any.

"Not at the moment. But do me a favor and don't leave town."

Mr. Morris smiled. "Whatever you say, Buster."

He gathered up his bucket and mop and started to walk away. With each step he made a jingling sound.

"Just a minute, Mr. Morris." Buster ran to catch up to him. "That jingling . . . It sounds like quarters. *A lot of quarters!*"

Mr. Morris pulled a huge key ring full of keys from his pocket. "I know what you mean," he said, jingling it. "I've often thought the same thing myself."

"Oh. Well, that's all right, then."

It wasn't really all right, thought Buster, at least not for Arthur. He had hoped to get to the bottom of the case quickly. But the more he dug, the more complicated the case became.

And the bottom was nowhere in sight.

Chapter 6
· · · · · · · · · · ·

I had been on the job a couple of hours, but aside from one cherry tart, I had little to show for it. Nobody was calling the suspect a liar, but nobody could support his story, either. I thought maybe a change of scene would help, so I made my way to the suspect's home. There I met up with the suspect's sister. She seemed to be a pretty cool customer, but I knew I could handle her.

"Come on, D.W., you must know *something.*"

They were standing in the Reads' kitchen. Arthur had gone out for a while, D.W. had said. But he couldn't go far, she figured. The police were probably watching the train and bus stations. "And his pictures are probably on Wanted posters by now," she said.

"D.W., I'm trying to clear Arthur, not send him to jail. Now think hard."

D.W. made a face. "All right, all right, I'll tell you what I know."

"Go on." Buster got out his pad and pencil.

"Ready? Okay, take this down. Every single word."

Buster nodded.

"THAT . . . HAT . . . LOOKS . . . SILLY . . . ON . . . YOU."

Buster put down his pencil. "This is serious, D.W. Besides, I like the hat."

D.W. giggled.

"Now back to the subject at —"

"What is this, Buster, the third degree? If I knew anything, I'd certainly tell . . . well, maybe not you. But somebody."

Buster pushed back his fedora. "Don't try that smoke screen stuff on me. I can see through you like a window. Now, think back to yesterday. Did Arthur bring home any big jingling bags . . . you know, absentmindedly?"

D.W. glared at him. "Buster, you're talking about my brother! He would never take other people's money and bring it home like that."

"Calm down, D.W. I don't think Arthur would do anything bad on purpose. But he could have been forgetful. I'm just checking out every possibility."

"Arthur's not that stupid," D.W. went on. Clearly, she had been giving the matter some serious thought. "He wouldn't just bring the money into the house. Too many questions to answer. Too many people might see it. But he'd want it close by. Hidden. Safe. But where? That's what I can't quite figure out. Not that Arthur's so clever. But still . . ."

She scratched her head.

"Of course!" she shouted. "We should check the lawn for signs of recent digging."

"But D.W. —"

She ran out the door. But before Buster could follow her, Arthur walked in.

"Oh, Buster! I'm glad you're here. Does this mean good news?"

"Sorry, Arthur. The case is still wide open."

Arthur sighed.

"I'm just trying to be thorough," Buster explained. "Detectives need to be thorough."

"Buster, if you don't find out who did it by tomorrow, I'll miss the picnic."

"I know. I haven't —"

He hesitated as D.W. passed by, carrying a shovel.

"Excuse me. Step aside. Coming through."

Arthur stared at D.W. and started to say something, but Buster held up his hand.

"You're better off not asking," he said. "You really don't want to know."

Chapter 7

●●●●●●●●●●●●

The situation did not look good. Everything still pointed to just one person — Arthur. Could he really be a criminal mastermind? I tried to picture him in his secret hideout, swimming in a sea of shiny quarters. They dripped through his fingers as he laughed insanely. Quarters! Quarters! He could never get enough.

Dinner at the Baxter house was quiet that evening. Mrs. Baxter was used to hearing Buster talk all about his day. But tonight Buster was quiet. Too quiet.

"Are you feeling all right?" his mother asked.

Buster nodded.

"But you've only had two helpings of dessert. That's not like you, Buster. You're sure you don't have a headache or fever?"

Buster shook his head. "It's just this case, Mom. I haven't figured out how to help Arthur yet."

"You're a good friend, Buster. I'm sure Arthur appreciates that."

"I hope so." But right now, thought Buster, Arthur needs more than a good friend. He needs a good detective.

Later, Buster sat at his desk, flipping through his pad. He was looking for clues, any clues that would help him solve the case. He wasn't feeling picky, either. Big clues, small clues, ragged-round-the-edges clues — Buster would have happily accepted *any* of them.

The phone rang.

"Buster, it's for you."

It was the Brain. He wondered if Buster was having any luck.

"Not yet," Buster reported.

"Well, keep trying. If I think of anything, I'll call you back."

A few minutes later, the phone rang again. This time it was Francine.

"Any progress?" she asked.

"No," said Buster.

"Okay. Keep me informed."

He had barely put down the phone when it rang again. Now Muffy was on the line. "It's too bad we can't buy clues," she said. "That would make things so much easier."

Buster agreed. But clues just weren't for sale.

After that the phone was quiet. Buster lay on his bed as a swirl of images — Mrs. MacGrady, Mr. Morris, and Arthur —

passed by in his mind. They were all involved somehow. He just had to put the pieces of the puzzle together.

"Buster, it's getting late!"

"I'm trying to crack the case."

"Well, you need your sleep, Mr. Detective. You're not a robot."

"You're right, I'm not a . . ." Buster leapt to his feet. "Robot! That's it! Mom, I love you!"

He went to the phone and dialed Arthur.

"Hello?" said Arthur.

"Great news!" shouted Buster. "I figured it out!"

"Really?" Arthur got all excited. "So, tell me."

"Okay. Well, the quarters were stolen by an army of evil robots. They need the metal for fuel. Nobody noticed them because they can transform themselves into . . . into . . . any shape."

Arthur sighed. "That's it? That's your big breakthrough?"

"Gosh, it sounded a lot better a minute ago. . . ."

"You'd better get some sleep," said Arthur.

"Okay," said Buster. "You too."

"I'll try," said Arthur. But if his only chance depended on finding an army of robots, he figured he was in for a long night.

Chapter 8

* * * * * * * * * * * *

Detectives are supposed to be tough, but even they feel the pain when a friend is hurting. And it was no different for me. I could tell from Arthur's eyes that he was not happy. Actually, I could tell from his mouth, the slump of his shoulders, even his ears. Arthur was a mess.

"Are you sure you want to be seen with me?" Arthur asked on the way to school the next morning.

"Of course," said Buster.

"People might begin to think you're my partner in crime. You could be my accomplice, my henchman, my —"

"Arthur, stop! Listen, I would never desert you. I'm no rat leaving a sinking ship. Why, even if you went to jail, I would write you. I would come visit. Well, you know . . ."

Buster realized this wasn't helping much. "Anyway," he added, "I'm really sorry you're going to miss the picnic today. And it's because I'm a bad detective. I know you're innocent."

Arthur tried to smile. "Thanks, Buster."

"I hate letting you down. If I just had a little more time."

"Forget it," said Arthur. "You did your best. You might be a lousy detective —"

"*Bad*, Arthur. I said *bad*."

"Oh, right. You might be a bad detective, but you're still a good friend."

Buster and Arthur soon arrived at school. Buster got in line for the picnic bus with the other kids.

Mr. Ratburn motioned to Arthur.

"Sorry about this, Arthur."

"Me, too, Mr. Ratburn."

His teacher nodded. "Don't give up. I'm sure the truth will come out in the end."

Arthur certainly hoped so.

"Children!" Mr. Haney shouted through his bullhorn. "Please board the school bus now."

Buster was standing with Binky and the Brain. They started to move forward.

"Poor Arthur," said the Brain.

"A good lawyer could get him off," said Binky. "They do it all the time."

"But Arthur's innocent," said Buster. "I just don't know how to prove it. The answer's somewhere right in front of me. Hey, what's that?"

He pointed to Binky's shirt.

Binky looked down. "Powdered sugar, I guess. I had a doughnut on the way to school."

"Oh. See, that's a clue. If this was the case of the missing doughnuts, I'd be all set." Buster frowned. "I just can't think straight anymore."

"I know how you feel," said the Brain. "Sometimes when I'm working on a tough math problem, I feel like my brain's overflowing with data."

"Keep it moving," said Mr. Haney.

Buster stepped onto the bus. Suddenly he stopped and stared at the Brain.

"Overflowing? Overflowing!"

"I think the pressure got to him," Binky whispered.

"That's it!" cried Buster. He shook the Brain's hand. "That's it!"

"What's it?" said the Brain.

Buster raced off the bus and almost ran into Mr. Haney.

"Hold on there, Buster. You're going the wrong way."

"Mr. Haney! I've solved the crime. Come on!"

Without waiting for an answer, he led the way into the school.

Chapter 9

· · · · · · · · · · ·

Every detective wants to be cool, calm, and collected at all times. And I was no different. But it's easy to say that while you're sitting back in your office with your feet up on the desk. It's another thing when you think you've saved your best friend from a fate worse than death.

In the kitchen, Mrs. MacGrady was packing up for the school picnic. She had the sandwiches, potato chips, and cartons of juice all neatly organized on the counter.

She was just getting ready to cut the sheet of brownies into squares when Buster rushed in. He was pulling Mr.

Haney behind him. "Slow down, Buster," said Mr. Haney. "We don't want to be arrested for speeding."

Mrs. MacGrady looked surprised. "Buster! Mr. Haney! What are you doing here?"

Mr. Haney cleared his throat. "Following up on a theory. Go ahead, Buster."

"Mrs. MacGrady, do you know why your brownie mix overflowed?"

"Not really. I don't mind saying it was a little embarrassing. But Mr. Morris was very nice about helping me clean it up."

"Has that ever happened before? The overflowing, I mean."

"No. I'm always very careful. But this time I guess I made too much."

"Did you use a different recipe?"

Mrs. MacGrady stopped to think. "Well, no, now that you mention it. The recipe was the same as always."

"Did you use any new equipment?"

Mrs. MacGrady laughed. "Not on my budget. I'm lucky they give me electricity."

Mr. Haney cleared his throat.

Buster picked up a knife and cut a square out of the brownie pan.

"And yet somehow something happened, something that had never happened before. Significant, don't you think?"

Mr. Haney folded his arms. "Buster, make your point, please. The bus is waiting."

Buster was getting to it. But detectives never rush their moments of glory.

"So you measured out the ingredients in the usual way. And you mixed them in the usual way. And yet something unusual happened. Shall I tell you why?"

Mrs. MacGrady smiled. "Please do."

"It's because you accidentally included one extra ingredient."

"I did?"

Buster nodded. He picked up the brownie and broke it in two.

A quarter fell out.

"Oh, my," said Mrs. MacGrady. "How did that happen?"

"It was Arthur," Buster explained. "You were on the phone when he came in. He thought you saw him, but you didn't. Then he left the bag of quarters next to the other ingredients. He had even spilled some of your flour on his bag, which is probably why you didn't notice."

Mrs. MacGrady broke open another brownie, and two quarters fell out.

"So now we know the truth," said Mr. Haney.

"Arthur is innocent!" Buster exclaimed. "It's time to set him free."

Chapter 10

One kind of detective fades back into the shadows once a case is solved. For that detective, solving the mystery is its own reward. He dodges the bright lights of the television cameras and the front page of the newspaper.

The other kind of detective likes to take a bow, to be recognized for doing good work. He doesn't duck the well-deserved compliment. I could see both sides, and I understood that some detectives would be shy about taking credit for untangling things.

But I wasn't one of them.

Arthur was sitting in detention alone with his thoughts. And at that particular moment, his thoughts were not very good company. The quarters were gone, and his reputation was in question. Even if he was someday proved innocent, he was still going to miss the third-grade picnic.

He could hear Miss Tingley typing in the next room. The clicking on the keyboard made Arthur think of crickets chirping. At least crickets were free to do what they wanted. They didn't have to worry about quarters or picnics or unexpected mysteries.

Suddenly Arthur heard another noise. This didn't sound like crickets at all. It sounded like *a lot* of people on the move.

Miss Tingley heard it, too. She stopped typing and got up to see what all the commotion was about.

It *was* a lot of people. The whole third

grade was coming down the hall. The students, the teachers, and even the bus driver were there.

"What's going on?" Miss Tingley asked.

"Stand back," Mr. Haney advised her. He opened the door to the room where Arthur was sitting. "Justice is about to be served."

"Arthur, I did it!" shouted Buster. "You're free."

Arthur stood up.

"I am? But how?"

"We've solved the mystery of the missing quarters," Mr. Haney explained. "They ended up in Mrs. MacGrady's brownies."

"Really?" said Arthur. He looked at Mr. Ratburn, who smiled at him.

"They must be the richest brownies she's ever made," said the Brain.

Everyone laughed.

"And," said Buster, "you owe it all to that great detective, that peerless investigator —"

Buster was cut off as Mr. Haney spoke into the bullhorn.

"Back to the bus, everyone!" he ordered. "The picnic awaits."

As the kids went back outside, Arthur shook Buster's hand.

"Thanks, Buster. I'm almost speechless. You're the best detective I know!"

"I'm the *only* detective you know."

"Well, yes, but you're still the best."

"If you say so."

"I do."

"All right."

He went on like that all the way out to the bus. I didn't try to stop him. A good detective knows when to sit back and listen.

The picnic was a big success. Later, though, Mrs. MacGrady faced a new mystery when a

plate of cookies she had put aside suddenly disappeared.

I brushed a few crumbs off my shirt and joined in the baseball game that was starting up. If Mrs. MacGrady wanted to solve that mystery, she was going to have to do it on her own.